Sheikha's Diary was authored by a Turkish novelist, educator, and mother. English storyteller, Ebru Alpsan writes for young readers. In her early years, Alpsan began to write short stories and poetry. Her tales make excellent metaphors for friendship, family, and self-awareness.

My book is dedicated to my students

Ebru Alpsan

SHEIKHA'S DIARY

AUSTIN MACAULEY PUBLISHERS™

LONDON • CAMBRIDGE • NEW YORK • SHARJAH

ISBN – 9789948760214 – (Paperback)
ISBN – 9789948760221 – (E-Book)

Application Number: MC-10-01-6362819
Age Classification: 6-9

First Published 2024
AUSTIN MACAULEY PUBLISHERS FZE
Sharjah Publishing City
P.O Box [519201]
Sharjah, UAE
www.austinmacauley.ae
+971 655 95 202

I want to thank my children, Zeynep and Omer not leaving me alone on my own adventure. Special thanks to two people who made this book more readable—Tarub Al Huleisy and Conor McHugh—and full support from friends. Friends become family.

September

It was the last few days of August before school started. I could hardly stay in my spacious green room. I cannot remember how often I wore my new pink school bag and read the name tag on my new copybook.

"Sheikha grade three."

I got out of the trance with the knock on my door.

"Sheikha, can I come in? I ironed your uniform," said Sanaya, my nanny from Sri Lanka.

Sanaya has deep-set round eyes, full lips, and a shy smile on her wrinkled face. Her wavy hair is always covered with a white scarf which I bought for her last year. She has glowing skin that varies from dark brown to light. My mom says she is family, but to me, she is a lady from Sri Lanka that came to cater to our needs. My needs that is.

Sanaya hung the ironed uniform on the handle of my wardrobe, patted my shoulder, and left the room. Before leaving the room, she murmured, "Go to bed now, I will wake you up for Fajr." (*The morning prayer*).

"Do I really have to get up? It's way too early!" I muttered.

"Of course you do, prayers only bring you closer to God," Sanaya responded gently.

"Arrrrgh," I mumbled.

Sanaya had this thing about her, no matter what I say or do, I find myself automatically agreeing to everything she asks me to do. I don't know if it was her over-the-top angelic voice or the fact that she bakes the best chocolate cake ever. I can't disagree with her and boy did I hate that.

I fell asleep that night, and you guessed it, I missed my Fajr prayer the next day. Don't get me wrong, I was not pleased with myself, but come on I am just a kid, God will forgive me, right?

It was almost six a.m.; my mother placed a glass of orange juice on the dresser next to my bed. She was all in a tizzy as she pulled the curtain open and let the morning sun flood the room.

"Sure," said my mom. "I will drop you at school, we will be late."

I dragged my tired self out of bed – still barely conscious – swiftly changed and went down for a fast breakfast that consisted of boiled eggs and freshly baked pita bread prepared by Sanaya.

My younger sister and I got in the car. From home to school, we listened to prayers and from time to time, I listened to my mother's pieces of advice. My heart was pounding fast as we came closer to the school. The cracks in the walls of the school can testify to how old that building is. It's even older than my late grandfather.

It has an open courtyard where we gather for morning assemblies. Grade threes, fours, and fives are on the second floor, all connected by long hallways.

My mom went to find my sister's classroom. Meanwhile, my eyes roamed the crowd in search of my best friend, Latifa.

There she was standing in front of the "Welcome Back" banner.

"Latifa!" I called out her name. I drew a shaky breath to calm myself and ran toward her with a sense of ease. I know Latifa since we were in kindergarten. She has thick, pitch-black braided hair that touches her hips. She hides her eyes behind her long eyelashes. She is the coolest person I have ever known. The exact opposite of me.

It was 7:30 a.m. The courtyard was full of students from different grades. Most of them were from last year's grade two classes, yet I had no idea who my classmates were and who the teacher would be.

The supervisor went on the stage with a bunch of papers in her hand. She invited all the other teachers on the stage. The teachers were holding the signs of their classes. Latifa and I were so excited to meet with our new teacher. I quickly took a glance at the signs raised up in the air. However, I still could not see the sign indicating where my class would be.

The supervisor announced the name, "Ms. Zoe, your class is waiting for you."

I knew that Ms. Zoe was our teacher. Her unique, shrill voice was heard from a distance.

"I am coming!" she said.

I heard her flat footfall on the staircase. She approached the stage with a broad smile on her face. Her white cheeks were blushed, and I could see the sprinkle of freckles over an upturned nose. I knew Ms. Zoe was our teacher before it was announced. I am not sure if it was her bubbly demeanor that gave it away. I was unsure of many things, but one thing I was sure of was that I would be loved and cared for. Weird, as I am not someone easily affected by emotions, or am I?

She went up the stage in two big steps, smiled at the teachers, and grabbed the class list from the supervisor's hand. It was our class, and I was right!

As we climbed the stairs behind our teacher, I questioned myself, "Will this be an amazing year?"

My Diary

It was not a spacious room for twenty students; on the contrary, it was a tiny class on the left side of the hallway. It was covered with calm pastel cardboards, which invited the most serene moments of the day. The wide-framed windows overlooking the sea from a distance were set deeply into the walls. A few pieces of interspersed class furniture around provide enough space to keep the books and the copybooks organized.

Bang! I heard the door close behind Ms. Zoe.

"Get ready for the first lesson, open your copybook and write the date," Ms. Zoe said briskly.

A brilliantly funny teacher who stays as polite and ingenious as ever.

From the very first moment, Ms. Zoe started setting the class routines. She always waited for us at the door with a broad smile on her face, then right away, she started her routine as if she was the commander of the class. I bet she knew that we liked to hear those sets of rules.

"Get the books."

"Write the date into your copybook."

"Grab a book from the library and start reading to your friend on the carpet until the bell rings."

Latifa and I sit in a group of three at the back of the class, close to the storage and lesson tools. Ahmad is the third person in our group. He tries to gain Ms. Zoe's favor. He pretends he is the big cheese in the class; however, Ms. Zoe is an impartial one. She always praises us for our enthusiasm to learn.

There is a horseshoe table in the middle of the class facing the whiteboard where Ms. Zoe supports the students who have difficulty in reading and writing. Salem has a spot on the right end of the horseshoe table next to the word wall. He likes to pile up his books in front of him like a castle to hide behind. As you can imagine, Salem is a slow reader but has a big imagination the fact that he blows up new characters from the stories pushes the lesson hilariously to a whole new level making us giggle every time.

On the other side of the class, another group of three is located opposite the computers. They call themselves "Brainy Badgers" and I can truly admit that they have the right to brag. Lilian is one of these two who is just a super-duper. She has an outstanding mathematical mind.

It was the last English lesson of the day. Ms. Zoe wrote the title of the lesson *Destiny's Gift*. As we started to read the story, I never thought it would be my favorite one. While we were reading and analyzing the lines, Ms. Zoe asked a very simple question in class, "Do you like your friends?"

First Ahmad answered as the walking encyclopedia of the class, "I like all my friends."

Salem swung on his chair and answered playfully, "I like them if they buy me gifts."

Latifa looked at me and said, "Sheikha is my best friend."

Lilian was waiting for the best moment to answer that simple question, "I love my friends, but I love my family more."

Ms. Zoe smiled and said, "Prove it to me."

"And also keep a diary for the year, write about your friends and the days in grade three."

Keeping a diary was a very new thing for me. I never write about my feelings; I always directly say them without any filter. Moreover, she wants us to prove our love to our friends.

How can I prove my love to my friend? I always love my family and friends, but nobody asked me to prove it until that moment. Ms. Zoe got the blue whiteboard pen from her drawer and wrote: "I will write a paragraph on friendship and read it to the class tomorrow."

Not gonna lie! It was a topic many of us would find difficult to write about, but it didn't bother me more than having the idea of keeping a diary.

As I was writing my homework on the board, I was also thinking about what to write and where to hide my diary.

When I was thinking about the diary, the highlights of my day would be the easiest way to start. Salem started counting back the last seconds of the lesson at the top of his voice. I could barely hear myself and the tick-tacking of the clock above the whiteboard. I packed my stuff and left the class in relief.

Best Friend

Latifa is my bestie. I think *best* is the perfect adjective that describes a friend. Our friendship started when we were five years old. Our mothers registered us for kindergarten on the same day. I went into the class with a burst of anger that caused a tantrum of kicking and screaming. She was sitting on a chair like a princess. She was wearing a tiered tulle dress in pink. She had two side braids frapped with white ribbons, and on the contrary, I had a messy bun on top.

The teacher called her name softly. "Latifa, please come here, hold the hand of Sheikha and show her the colors."

She approached me cautiously and wanted to hold my hand; yet I roared so wildly that she had to step back.

"It is okay!" she said softly. "Your mother will come soon." I believe she could not stand my sulkiness anymore, so she told me the BEST lie ever. And it worked!

The first year of kindergarten passed so quickly. The summer break was around the corner, and all the kids in the class were happy except me. I liked to brag about my masterpieces dangling in the hallway. Although I call them masterpieces, they were like some creatures coming from space. Latifa was the only one who always showed her admiration for my coloring by opening her big, black eyes wide and clapping her hands.

I can admit that sometimes her calmness and positivity was hitting a nerve in me, but she was my BEST friend.

It was the second year of kindergarten. Latifa and I had a big fight. I pulled her braids and broke her hairpin. It was a sunny day, and our teacher, Ms. Noor, took us outside to the swings. Latifa did not like to swing on the monkey bars in the grassy area. On the contrary, I liked to jump, hop, and climb. Unlike me, her hobbies were colors and playing with her jewelry.

I have no idea how many minutes I played with the other boys. I suddenly jumped out of the swing, ran toward her, pushed her with all my strength, and made her fall. I think all I wanted was to have a good time with her in the playground. She started crying; however, it was not my last strike. I pulled her thick braided hair and broke her favorite hairpin. Yes, it was her favorite hairpin because I had the same one.

She did not talk to me for three days. It was so clear that everyone in the class was on her side. It was the third day; I flounced into the classroom, threw myself, possibly a little too hard onto the bean bag chair, fell out of my place, and started crying. She came, held my hand as if it was the first day of kindergarten, and said, "It is okay. You only missed where you need to sit."

It was such a silly conversation, yet it made us laugh loudly. Since then, "laughing" has become the only way to make peace between us.

Years passed, and I am in grade three now. I learned from her to look at the problems from different windows. This is a bit annoying getting some life lessons from your peer but in the end, she is my best friend.

We never keep secrets from each other; however, I got the sense that something was wrong that week. Ms. Zoe distributed the registration papers for the next year. She reluctantly took the paper and put it into her bag. I returned the signed paper the next day; however, she did not. I did not think too much of it, but when I saw her crying secretly in the courtyard, it was my bottom line.

I curiously asked, "What is bothering you this much?"

The other girls immediately huddled around to learn the reason; however, I gave them an angry look, and they hardly found a reason to stay there.

Latifa could not hold herself more, she poured all her anger and sorrow out. Her parents decided to transfer her to another school close to the house.

It was the worst news ever.

"Do not be silly! They can't," I said bewilderingly.

"I feel so wretched." She was sobbing hysterically.

It was the first time I saw my best friend crying loudly. Yes! We had miserable days, but that moment was the worst.

I went home in desperation, threw my heavy body to my bed, and started punching my pillow. My mom tried to cheer me up by bringing me a glass of hot chocolate, but my response was a wild look saying, "Seriously! This is what you can do?"

"You will have a lot of best friends, don't worry," she said.

Her sentence was even worse than the glass of hot chocolate.

"Boohoo, you don't care about me at all. Please call her mother."

She left the room silently, leaving me alone.

I fell asleep in anger. I woke up after an hour. I overheard my father talking with someone on the phone.

He said, "We will pick her up every morning and drop her home after school."

I sluggishly went out of the room.

"Who are we picking every morning?" I asked.

"You want us to do something for Latifa, right?" said my mother.

"Latifa's father is getting a new job in Abu Dhabi, so he needs to leave the house early in the morning that's why they want to send her to a close-by school," said my mother.

"But not fair!" I reacted angrily.

"Well, your father solved the problem for you. We will pick her up every morning and drop her."

I looked at my father.

"Seriously!" I exclaimed.

He nodded.

I hopped up to my father's shoulders, exulted at our victory.

I was on the phone with Latifa until late that night, planning for the things we would do on the school way.

When I was writing the last words of my diary, I felt so lucky that I have a best friend who accepts me as I am but also helps me to become who I should be.

Spelling Bee – May

I had practiced the sounds and the words a thousand times that week. No joke! Yes, in every single break, I practiced the Spelling Bee words because it was my goal to be the winner of grade three.

The word echoed in my ears as I was anxiously waiting in the bumble bee-decorated library.

"Together, together," repeated Ms. Zoe.

I repeated the word quietly and wrote *something* down. It was the first round of the spelling competition, and it was the beginning of an end.

On the same morning of the Spelling Bee, Sanaya called me down for breakfast.

The smell of freshly baked pita bread made me bounce down the stairs.

"**br Ek fUHst,**" I spelled the word. My nanny, Sanaya repeated the word after me hilariously.

"bir ak fahst," she said.

Her Sri Lankan accent made me smile, I laughingly corrected her mistake.

"Break-fast silly! not brakfahst,"

"My "**st UH mUHk**" hurts," I said grumpily.

Spelling the conversation sounds weird yet it was also so cool to be understood by a few people around. It was like a secret language and only a few people know.

She looked at my mom to analyze what I was talking about.

Mom said sloppily, "Stomach."

Mom is not a morning person. She was busy with her Turkish coffee so my spelling practice was not her concern at that time of the day.

It was a morning with a lot of spelling, Mom seemed a bit cross, so she decided to drop us at school earlier than our usual time.

I spelled whatever I saw through the window on the way to school.

As I was practicing, I did not know that I scattered all the papers in the back. Mom was clearly upset with the mess; she murmured a prayer with a head shake.

Finally, I was at school, jumped out of the car, and rushed to the class.

Latifa was humming the sounds of each word silently.

Ahmad was writing the words on small pieces of paper. There was no way better than writing to memorize so many words.

Lilian and her two brainy ones, Noora and Wadima, were in a small competition.

Salem kept the door ajar with one foot inside, annoying the other students passing in front of our class. He exclaimed with excitement, "Ms. Zoe is coming!"

He rushed back to his place, crossed his arms, and pretended that he was waiting passionately.

Ms. Zoe reached her place in five long steps and asked us to go to the library and get ready for the first round of the Spelling Bee competition.

She put the papers and her pink glasses on top of the paper pile. She grabbed one sheet among the bunch; meanwhile, I could picture the words in my head, which was easy for me.

My hands were shaking, and I could hear the drumbeat of my heart. All the sounds of the alphabet were running through my head.

Ms. Zoe read nineteen words. I wrote down all the words carefully. When she read the last one, I knew I would make a mistake. I repeated the word "misbehave" but I wrote "together" and put the pencil down. I looked at Latifa. She was biting her lips and holding her fingers tightly.

Ahmad yawned loudly and cracked his fingers. He buzzed in my ear, "Piece of cake."

"How did it go?" Ms. Zoe asked.

"Well, as usual, perfect!" said Ahmad.

"All done," said Saif boastfully. He knew he did not do well.

"What about you, Sheikha?" Ms. Zoe asked.

"Do you think one letter word might change everything?" I asked. I know it was not the answer to her question, but I believe one word would change the result of the competition.

Somehow, I knew she would tell me what I didn't want to know.

She smiled and collected all the papers.

It was almost dismissal time; we were all waiting eagerly to hear about the winners of the first round.

Mrs. Zoe came inside the class with a paper in her hand. As she was unfolding the paper to announce the names, a prolonged silence in the class followed her actions.

Lilian leaned back in her place with her eyes closed. Latifa held my hand tight and whispered, "Oh God! I want to win, please."

I could not tell her how much I wanted to win the first round of the Spelling Bee when I saw her praying.

"Well, I am very proud of you, all of you did a great job." She continued, "But we need to choose the BEST three spellers."

"Salama, you are the first speller. Ahmad, you are the second speller," Ms. Zoe declared.

Salama and Ahmad exclaimed, "Yippee!"

Who was the third name? It was the longest minute of the lesson. Salama and Ahmad were already jumping in their places! Maybe Ms. Zoe announced the third name, but I could not hear it.

"Latifa, you are the third BEST speller," Ms. Zoe said.

I felt happiness and jealousy at the same time. I wanted to cry while laughing with my friend. If Latifa is the BEST, am I the WORST?

That night I thought about it a lot. I knew I was not the worst, but I wanted to hear it from someone. Latifa is my friend, I should be happy for her. At the same time, we were in a competition, and she was my rival.

Latifa called me late at night. She asked me to help her with the second round.

"You are one of the super students in the class and I cannot do this without your help," she said.

Have you ever seen a smiling monkey in your life? Yup! It was me after her call. It made me so proud of myself that I started spelling whatever I saw in the house. Yes, I could not wing the spelling bee, and yes, maybe I am not the BEST speller in the competition, but I am one of the best students in the class who learned from her mistakes and learned to spell the word "together" correctly.

Believe in Yourself

One, two, three run! I ran to the wall of the living room, touched it with all my effort, and shouted with triumph, "I beat you! I beat you. Yay!" My sister started crying but who cares, I bounced on the sofa hopping from one corner to another.

I heard Mom's angry voice from the kitchen, "Sheikha! Enough, leave your sister alone, you always make her cry." It was not an unusual thing in the house; however, I was training for Sports Day.

It is not the longest marathon in the country, but Sports Day is the most fun day in the school in which all of us compete till we lose our last breath.

Our PE teacher, Mr. Finn is from Ireland. Everyone can hear his whistle when he blows it from the stairs. It means lining up outside the classroom. On that day, Mr. Finn organized all grade three teachers to prepare the banners. Ours was a tiger. We started decorating the banner with glitter and colors a few days before the computations. It was a yellow tiger banner. Ms. Zoe picked me and Ahmad as the responsible coach.

"Please help all the girls, especially Noora," she said.

Noora was the slowest in the class. She had some balance problems while walking. Her fragile, short legs did not help her walk straight. Noora had to wear some special shoes clicking on her each step which helped her walk straight.

I got the order from Ms. Zoe and started to train the girls for the games. I took the task so seriously that I did not let the girls have any free time during recess but had them run from one corner to another in the courtyard. I trained them so hard that the class bell turned into salvation for them. It was not training but torture. While I was running with the girls, Ahmad was also coaching the boys' team. We come together from time to time to have top confidential meetings on the strategic games we would play during Sports Day.

Ahmad and I announced the names according to the pupil's speed.

"Thani and Lilian will be the first," I said.

"Latifa and Salim will run after," Ahmad said.

Ahmad and I will be the last runners after fifteen students. "What about me?" Noora asked.

Noora was looking at me with begging eyes asking me to cut her name from the list.

"Noora, you will carry the banner and you will compete in the egg and the spoon race."

Well, the only thing we needed for that game was the balance, and Noora's clicking shoes would help us to win.

On the day of the Sports Day, we all lined up outside and waited for Ms. Zoe to come. Noora was holding the banner. I had been an enthusiastic cheerleader with a loud voice coming from my throat. We started to chant.

"Tiger is gonna win."

"Shout it to the East."

"Shout it to the West."

"We are the best, we are gonna win!" Ahmad was prancing and hopping in front of the crowd escorting the teacher.

The game started with the whistle of Mr. Finn. All students from different sections were competing to death.

We could not do much in the sack race and the tug of war. I ran back and forth checking and encouraging the girls and so did Ahmad. We were losing the game, and all of us were so exhausted to do better than we were doing and only one game was left behind to decide on the winner of the games. Egg and the spoon race.

Ahmad and I ran back to Noora. She was hiding behind the tiger banner.

"Come on, Noora, it is your turn," Ahmad said.

"Please, skip me. I cannot," Noora said.

"Don't be scared, it is a game," Lilian said.

She reluctantly held the spoon and the egg and started walking to the starting line. Her shoes were clicking with each step as if we were in the war and combat boots were marching.

There were three sets in the race. The first race was only ten steps. She passed that level.

The second set was walking on a bumpy road with the spoon in the mouth. She did it well too.

We were all clapping, shouting, hopping, and cheering her name.

"Noora, Noora."

"One last game," Ahmad said.

"I am tired, and my feet are hurting," Noora said.

"You can do it," Salem said punching the air.

Her heart was beating like a drum and her usually pale face was like lava out of a volcano.

Mr. Finn blew the first whistle and all the competitors took their places. Her feet were trembling.

We all gathered behind her, cheering her name.

The five competitors started walking with the second whistle. The first dropped the egg, and the second one followed her. The third racer twisted his ankle and left the game.

Noora and the next-class racer were very close to the finish line. It was a close fight. The only thing we heard was the clinking braces in her shoe. Noora got a big step and reached the line. She was like in slow motion running towards a finish line.

Mr. Finn whistled, and the game was over.

"Hurray!" screamed all the boys.

We ran to her cheering her name.

Ms. Zoe gave her a big hug. "You did a great job, the best game ever."

"Thank you," she replied.

"OMG! Noora, seriously, without you, we could not beat them," Latifa said.

Mr. Finn gave medals to all the grade three students for our sportsmanlike behavior and the big cup to Noora.

We came back to our class, exhausted but very proud.

Ms. Zoe lauded us as a great team.

The only thing I remember from that day was clicking the braces of Noor's shoes. Click and click sound of the shoes brought us success, pride, and unity.

The bell rang; Noora wore her backpack, and as she was walking slowly out of the class, her tiny legs were not helping her anymore. I grabbed her backpack and gave my arm to her. As we were leaving the class silently, I heard her tiny voice, "Thank you for everything."

The Blue

It was spring break. I did not do much instead of chatting with Latifa on the phone and gossiping about the girls in the class.

The girls created a chat group and shared their silly pictures and recordings of their singing. I was tired of listening to the messages coming back-to-back, yet I did not have much to do.

After two weeks of torture staying home and wandering from room to room, we finally started school. On the first day of the second term, I said bye to my mom in the car, slammed the door hard, and did not even look back at whether my mom was furious or not.

Ms. Zoe took attendance as usual at 7:40. As I said before, she has a routine to follow every day. She comes to the class, puts her books on her desk, takes her place in front of the whiteboard, and peers over her pink reading glasses to count the students.

That day she did something different. She took her place in the middle of the class and read the attendance list.

"Lilian," she called out.

"Here," Lilian said.

"Ahmad."

"Yep! Here I am."

"Sheikha."

"Present."

"Sai? Is Sai here?" she asked.

"Sai! Who is Sai?" I questioned.

"The new student," Ms. Zoe said. "She is from China."

"Eh?" I said.

"Cool," Latifa said. "I never had a Chinese friend before. I am so excited."

Ms. Zoe continued. "Good to hear this, Latifa. When she comes, please help her to learn the names. It is a new country and culture, might be a bit scary for her."

"No worries! Ms. Zoe, we will do our best," said Latifa, and all the girls echoed at once.

I rolled my eyeballs and itched my head. Latifa kicked me with her elbow. Whoever knows me well knows that if I itch my head, it means I am not happy. An unexpected girl from another country threw me into confusion.

That day, all our conversations were mainly about the new girl from China.

Lilian immediately went through the web pages to learn the meaning of her name, and Wadima looked up the dictionary and learned how to say "good morning" in Chinese.

When Ms. Zoe gave a chance to her to answer any question, she first said, "Zǎoshang hǎo," which means good morning in Chinese; then she answered the questions, and this continued until the dismissal. One good thing from that day was that the class learned to greet each other, even if it was in Chinese.

The next day in the English lesson, our section supervisor, Ms. Sawsan, came inside the class with Sai. She was hiding behind Ms. Sawsan's abaya. She was almost 4.5 feet, with silky black medium-length hair tucked behind her ear. Her short bangs covered half of her brow. I saw her clear face when Ms. Sawsan introduced her to us.

"Please meet Sai," Miss Sawsan said and continued. "I am sure everyone will help her." Then she exclaimed by looking at me, "I said, everyone!" I assume she expected a "big yes" from me; however, I could not do more than a nod.

Latifa loved Sai's blue hairband and the blue socks. She cheerily asked Ms. Zoe to add her to our group. Although I gave her shoulder a nudge, she ignored me and put her chair beside mine.

Sai was quite shy, avoided eye contact, and was not talking as much as the other girls. It was a good thing for me: less talk, less trouble.

In all lessons, Ms. Zoe gave her less work and more time to complete it. "It is not fair," I murmured.

Latifa hushed me. "Sai will hear you, and she will be unhappy."

"I do not care and don't want her on our team," I said.

Ms. Zoe heard what I said and gave me a frowny face. I grabbed my sticky notepad and wrote angry messages to Latifa, blaming her for bringing Sai to our team.

The girls added her name to our chat group, and she got the nickname "The Blue." Her blue socks and hairband made me up for that nickname.

That year, Hag Al Laila fell on Friday. I was so excited; Ms. Zoe would give us sweets and treats. I bet it would be a day with surprises.

I dressed in my traditional clothes for school and carried a bag of candies to class. Latifa's thrive was not different from mine. The distinctive clickety-clank sound of our necklaces could be heard from a distance while we were running in the hallway. It was time for the girls to show off, except for The Blue. She was in the class alone, waiting for Ms. Zoe to come inside the class.

Ms. Zoe appeared in the hallway carrying a basket full of colorful packages. All of us ran to her, trying to get her attention and excited to learn what she was carrying.

Ms. Zoe usually speaks loudly and quickly, but that time her voice was weak; it was evident that something had happened that morning. She used a smooth, controlled gesture to direct us to our places. She raised her shoulders toward her ears, rolled them back, and dropped them with a deep breath.

She gave sweets to everyone except Blue and me. Boys in the corner were already biting sweets and constantly licking their lips. Most of them finished their candies and some of them wiped their lips on their sleeves. I was shocked, and tens of questions passed through my mind about the reason why Ms. Zoe skipped me.

Latifa and Lilian gently opened the candy wrappers and put the lollipops in their mouth.

"Where is my candy? Ms. Zoe," I asked.

"You are not getting a treat, but I am giving you and Sai a packet of seeds. Both of you will plant the seeds, and I will give your gift at the end," Ms. Zoe said.

What seeds she was talking about? My cheeks were flushed, and I hardly controlled my anger and held back my tears. I got permission for the toilet and left the class.

I threw the packet of seeds to the floor in the toilet. Seeds were scattered around. I stepped on them angrily. I could have stepped on all if Latifa had not come after me. Latifa collected a few seeds from the floor and put them in a clean tissue, calmed me down, and dragged me to the class.

"I know you are upset now, but you will understand me later. Please go down to the planting area and plant the seeds," Ms. Zoe said firmly.

Sai and I went down to the planting area. We got a shovel and a pot of water. I did not even look at her face or say a word. On the contrary, she was so happy and dancing on her tiptoe. It was the first time I saw her enjoying her time. We watered the seed for ten days. Finally, the seed blossomed. I was so delighted when I saw the seedlings emerge from the soil. We started to dance around the young flower.

"Let's give a name to this flower," said Sai.

"I never thought of a name. What do you think?"

"Happy," said Sai. "We call it Happy."

I giggled. "Do not be silly. Who calls a flower Happy."

"I want to call it 'happy' because you are my first friend, and you make me happy." She repeated the word 'happy' for a few times flipping her hands.

That white flower was a bond between Sai and me and it made me smile all day long.

The next day, Sai was absent, and the next day too. I was so worried but could not ask anyone about her. I went down to the planting area and watered our "Happy" flower every day. It was a beautiful white flower. After two days, Ms. Zoe entered the class with a woman and Sai. Sai was holding her hand. This time she was wearing white socks and a white hairband.

Ms. Zoe introduced Sai's mother to us. The lady approached me slightly, embraced me, and said, "Thank you,

you did a great job." I was really surprised by that big hug but blushed, stumbling over my words.

"It is okay, it was just a flower."

Ms. Zoe continued, "Do you know what Sai means in Chinese?"

Wadima answered proudly, "I know how to say good morning in Chinese. But I don't know the meaning of her name."

Ms. Zoe continued, "It means white flower, and Sheikha, you helped Sai to blossom again." I blushed at the unexpected compliment.

Sai's mother gave me a box of sweets. My eyes were wild open. "But this is too many," I exclaimed with joy.

"You deserve it; share it with your friends," she said.

Everyone gathered around me to get one, but I kept the biggest ones for Latifa and Sai.

I Am Thankful

We huddled around the table, waiting for the Imam to start the prayer. The time was stubborn to pass. I could finally hear the clock's tic-tacks, three seconds, two seconds, and one. With the prayer, we all started Ramadan. Ramadan has been the most joyous month of the year for me. My mother always prepares food for the needy people around our house. My grandad calls us around him after iftar and hypnotizes us with his stories. This pattern continues for thirty days.

My sister started eating so fast that I had to kick her under the table, but instead of slowing her eating pace, she said, "Ow, why'd you kick me." I rolled my eyeballs, pretending I did nothing.

No joke! My sister finished her plate in five minutes and started nagging about her stomach cramps. "What on earth are you doing? You know you need to eat slowly and less," I said.

She shrugged her shoulder and sat next to my grandmother on the brownish sofa putting her head on her lap.

It was a busy night. My mom and I put up lights on the wall and decorated the living room with colorful lanterns, which gave a holy and magical atmosphere. My sister did not even move from her place, but she was an expert at giving us orders from her comfy spot. We went to bed late and I immediately slept off exhaustion.

The next day I woke up to my sister's scornful words. "Yuk! You are drooling. You smell bad."

"Leave me alone," I said and covered the blanket over my head.

"Momma," my sister yelled, "Sheikha does not wake up."

"She is lying," I answered back. "I already woke up."

"Go out of the room," I growled.

She ran out of the room with a sneaky smile.

My mother called out, "Hurry up! I need to drop you at school, I have many things to do."

The school was quieter than usual. Latifa was waiting for me in the courtyard. She hugged me and whispered into my ear, "Happy Ramadan."

Mustafa was hanging some Ramadan decorations on the reception ceiling and welcoming everyone.

Mustafa has been working for our school for ten years. He is everything to our teachers.

"Mustafa, I need paper." "Mustafa, I need a board marker." And many more can be heard in a day.

He is a thin and tall man in his 40s. He is brownish and has a broad smile. He always wears a white shirt and black trousers with brown slippers. Like the others, he sends money to his family in Pakistan.

We were in the class waiting for Ms. Zoe to take attendance. Ms. Zoe said, "Morning everyone, and happy Ramadan."

Salem started nagging, "My stomach is growling. How many hours do we have?"

Ahmad giggled. "Eight hours."

"OMG!" he said.

Ms. Zoe started talking about why we should be thankful and merciful. She said, "Be proactive, not reactive. Let's change some people's lives."

Latifa asked, "What do you mean by being proactive?"

Lilian said, "We are still kids."

I was trying to read Ms. Zoe's mind. Then a light bulb went off in my head, and I said, "We should help people."

"This is what I was thinking," said Ms. Zoe.

Our social lesson teacher, Ms. Rodha, joined our lesson. "Ah! Good, you started talking about the project."

Ms. Rodha always comes to class with big ideas. Her lessons are always fun and exciting. She included our class in her project, which made me thrilled.

Ms. Rodha continued, "We will open a small market in the school."

I said, "I will sell my sister's toys." I know it would create trouble at home; at least it would be a chance for me to take revenge for this morning.

Ms. Zoe added, "Sheikha, you don't need to sell your sister's toys. We can sell our used books and homemade cookies."

"Selling my sister's toys would give me a different joy than selling the old books or cookies," I mumbled.

Salem asked, "What will we do with the money?"

Ms. Rodha continued, "You will buy food for the staff who are helping the teachers."

With one voice, we called out, "Mustafa."

Ms. Zoe said, "Not only Mustafa, but we also have two more people helping the teachers, and we need to help them in Ramadan."

That was the plan. Bake, collect the money, and give!

That night we were all swamped with phone calls and baking.

Morning time, my nanny filled the car with cupcakes. Freshly baked cupcakes.

When we reached school, Ms. Zoe and Ms. Rodha had already set the courtyard's tables and decorations. Mustafa was helping them, not knowing the reason for that organization. My mother and I carried the trays of cupcakes. The girls brought their used, old books. They sorted the books out according to their cover colors. Black books were in the bottom left corner, red and yellow were in the top right corner, and the colorful, thin ones were in the middle. They put the price tags on each.

Ms. Zoe said, "The books will be for five dirhams only."

Salem and Ahmad were planning to sell the books more expensive, but Ms. Rodha gave them a look, and they could not even intend to change the tag.

The recess time was the sale time. All the teachers and the supervisors came to buy the cupcakes. While Latifa was selling the cupcakes, I was counting the money we had collected. Salem pointed to the cupcakes. "Spare me the biggest cupcake; I will eat it after iftar." He was hardly talking with his drooling mouth.

At the end of the recess, we saved a good amount of money for three people.

"We did it!" said Lilian.

Latifa clapped her hands with joy.

"You can't change many things at your age, but you can put a smile on a person's face," Ms. Zoe said proudly.

We divided the money into three and put them into colorfully decorated envelopes.

Ms. Rodha called Mustafa and the other two assistants to our class. Ms. Zoe asked me to give the envelopes. I cheerfully accepted and got my place with my teachers.

I could see the joy in their eyes while I was handing in the embroidered envelopes. Ms. Zoe and Ms. Rodha thanked Mustafa and the other assistants for their help and wished them a happy Ramadan.

Mustafa said, "I will send this money to my child in Pakistan so that she can buy the dress she wants to wear on Eid."

Latifa and I looked at each other. We were proud of ourselves. I was so thankful to be a part of this classroom and grateful to have my family by my side.

That iftar was different from the others. I sat in between my grandfather and father and talked about our project at school. It was the first time in my short life I realized how thankful I am to be the daughter of my father. I constantly watched him while we were having our iftar.

It was time for bed when I saw Granny bring us warm milk.

"Pray for everyone, God will answer your prayers," she said.

That night I prayed more than I usually do. I prayed for my family, teachers, Mustafa, and that small Pakistani girl waiting for her father.

Change

The morning sun passed through the curtain and hit my face. I was ready to leave my dark green room for the last day of school. I gazed at my reflection in the floor mirror in the corner.

The usual messy bun on my head did not seem right to me this time. I quickly unleashed it, comped my hair neatly, and had two braids instead. I am sure this change would surprise my friends and family because I was already bewildered by what I just did. No lies! I liked my new hairstyle more.

My mom saw me from the rear mirror of the car and murmured audibly so that I could hear her curiosity.

But I ignored what I heard and pretended as if nothing was unusual.

The school was another story. I steadily went to my place passing in in front of curious looks and sat quietly in the class.

Ahmad intended to open his mouth.

"Do not even dare," I said hastily.

"Is everything all right?" asked Lilian.

"MYOB," I sulkily said.

It was the last week of school. We finished all the exams and Ms. Zoe was talking about grade four lessons.

I was excited for the next year, yet growing, changing, and even saying goodbye to my friends and Ms. Zoe was the hardest part of the year.

That day girls gathered at the corner of the class. Latifa brought letter beads and colorful cotton strings to do friendship bracelets.

"Very girly stuff," I said irrelevantly, yet I wanted to have one.

I said, "Hey Latifa, make me a blue one."

Latifa did not say anything. She pretended as if it was my usual request.

"Great choice, Sheikha. I will make the same for me."

The other girls looked at each other with wild eyes open but Latifa hushed them and started my blue bracelet with agility.

Ms. Zoe came and sat next to me.

"You look so beautiful, Sheikha."

"Thank you, Ms. Zoe; I wanted to have a change."

"Good decision. I liked this change."

"It seems you are growing."

"Growing and changing. Am I ready for this change?" I whispered to her.

Ms. Zoe has magical words. The way she explains any question always mesmerizes us.

"You are ready for any change; you are brave enough to stand on your own feet." She patted my shoulder.

I knew I am brave and can do anything, yet I wanted to hear it from Ms. Zoe. Her words always encouraged me to do better.

While I was fighting with my emotions, Latifa briskly brought the blue friendship bracelet.

"Here you go." It was a zipper look beaded bracelet made from three neon blue strings, attached a large knot at the top of the bracelet, and the word "Be Brave" was dangling at the edge of it.

Ms. Zoe got it smiling and said, "This is what we were just talking about." And tied the bracelet to my wrist.

The recess bell brought me back to reality from my gloomy thoughts. My stomach was roaring with hunger and when I am hungry, I cannot function.

I said, "Well, I don't know about you guys, but I am starving because I did not eat much in the morning. Let's go to the courtyard."

Ahmad asked, "Are you done with your diary?" It was the weirdest question asked just before I was leaving for the breakfast break.

I snapped at him, "I am starving. I don't know about you, but I can't think on an empty stomach, and I am done with my diary."

Ahmad did not even wait for me to finish my words and ran away to catch the other boys.

As I mentioned before, Ms. Zoe asked us to keep a diary for the year. It was an assignment for us then it turned into a habit and a secret friend for me. It was almost the end of the year and I did not know how to complete my last words about grade three, my friends, and my teacher.

We went out to the yard and had a potluck. Lucky me! Take one piece from everyone and your boring cheese sandwich turns into a feast.

Latifa quietly sat by me and whispered, "I heard Ms. Zoe will be our teacher for next year."

"What!"

"Yes, I overheard her talking."

"OMG! Latifa, this is the best news."

"Shh, you are too loud."

"Okay, okay!" I said jumping in my place.

It was so difficult for me to hide my joy from the others in the class, even from Ms. Zoe.

It was the last period of the year. Ms. Zoe gave us the topic, "Choose your own adventure and write your story."

I immediately opened my diary to write about the conclusion of my story.

I started writing about my adventure – goodbye to my messy bun, my rowdy behavior, and my desk at the back of the class. I had fears before but now, I have plans. I am thriving and this does not scare me. While I was writing these lines, the letter beads on my bracelet caught my eye. "Be Brave" and this is all we need to continue our journey. I put my pencil down and closed the diary. I went to Ms. Zoe's desk and gave her a big, tight hug. It was a hug that I have never given to anybody.

"Thank you, Ms. Zoe, for helping me to write about my own adventure." She smiled back. With each passing minute, the children became more anxious, waiting for the final school bell. Three seconds, two, and one screamed at one voice and the bell was heard.

I grabbed my bag and left the class with joy.

www.ingramcontent.com/pod-product-compliance
Lightning Source LLC
Chambersburg PA
CBHW021403160726
47994CB00007B/3055